Hearts United In Love

Hearts United, Volume 2

Karen Kazimer Shockley

Published by Karen Shockley, 2024.

HEARTS UNITED IN LOVE

First edition. July 8, 2024.

ISBN: 979-8227994431

Written by Karen Kazimer Shockley.

Table of Contents

To Those Who Have Experienced the

Trials of Love and Marriage

Before this story begins

Daniel, a devoted father, is left to raise his two young children after his wife succumbs to breast cancer. Meanwhile, Rachel, a widowed mother, grapples with her own grief and loss of faith after her husband is tragically killed.

Through chance and divine intervention, their paths cross, leading to a beautiful journey of love, understanding, and healing. As Daniel and Rachel navigate the challenges of single parenthood and their contrasting beliefs, they discover that love and faith can unite even the most broken hearts.

They marry and join their families. Daniel with his two children, Sandra and Michael, and Rachel with her daughter, Amy, blend together in a truly blessed experience.

Unsettling Adjustments

Rachel

I pulled out an empty suitcase and turned to my wardrobe. "Uhhh!" I murmured, raising both hands in the air. I was furious. At myself, at Daniel, at this whole situation.

Tears blurred my vision as I yanked open the wardrobe doors and began pulling out armfuls of my clothes, flinging them on the bed with so much vehemence that one would think they'd been the ones who'd offended me.

This is absolutely awful! I can't believe this is happening to me. Life is just not fair!

Shaking all over, I crammed blouses, pants, dresses into the open suitcase sitting on the comforter, not even bothering to fold them.

I felt I had to get out before I completely suffocated. I ran into Amy's room, grabbed an armful of her clothes, then hurried back to fling them into the suitcase. The case was stuffed full in minutes. With piles of clothes on the bed and the floor, I dragged another case out from the closet, flung it open and continued to fill it with outfits.

I was not even registering what I was packing through the rage flooding every fiber of my being. How had it come to this - shoving everything I owned into suitcases like my house was on fire?

Daniel had abandoned me, leaving me alone to raise three kids. Two of these children weren't even mine. I furiously swiped at my wet cheeks as I forced the overflowing suitcases to close and yanked at the zips. The kids would be home from school in an hour, and I needed to be gone by then.

Our next door neighbor volunteered to watch them until she could contact Daniel and he could make other arrangements. I just needed to gather essential documents and a few cherished photos. Then I could disappear, leaving all this stress behind me for good.

They'd be better off without me. I always fell short, no matter how hard I tried. I was the woman who gave everything she had, and yet it was never enough. At this point, it seemed like it never would be and the best choice I had was to escape before I shattered completely.

My heart raced with adrenaline and sorrow as I scrawled a quick note for Daniel. He might worry when he found it, but my needs mattered, too. For once, I had to find a way to finally put myself first, again. It was time to stop the endless endurance contest.

As I reached for the door handle, my gaze caught the photo of us on the mantle. Daniel had his arm wrapped around me. Both of us were smiling at the camera. He looked so handsome; his warm brown eyes crinkled at the corners. In the picture, I was looking up at him, my eyes filled with love.

How happy I used to be with Daniel. I looked forward to living with him, forever. Looking at him now, I remembered why I had fallen for him. He was full of kindness and integrity. His calm nature perfectly settled my more flammable temperament. The tears flowed faster as I studied our smiling faces. *We'd been so happy. Where had things gone wrong? When did this bone-deep exhaustion and despair become my constant companions?*

I tore my eyes away, grabbing the handles of the overstuffed suitcases. I would have to pick up Amy from school, and we needed to be gone before I had to answer any questions from Sandra and Michael.

Especially Michael. *What could I possibly tell Michael that he'd understand?* I swiped at another tear, my mind racing as I tried to figure out where we would go.

Maybe my late husband's mother would take us in for a bit. Or I could drain my meager savings on a motel room. My options weren't that tempting, but I just knew I had to get away from this crushing stress and loneliness.

My phone vibrated angrily in my pocket. Taking it out, I saw Daniel's handsome visage flash across the screen. I silenced the call and shoved it back in my pocket. I was not ready to speak to him yet. There were too many angry sobs building in my chest. But Daniel persisted in trying to reach me, and the phone kept buzzing.

Finally, I gave in and answered, my voice sharp. "Daniel. Not right now. Please." "Rachel?" His warm, concerned tone only made me cry harder. "What's going on? I've been trying to call, but it keeps going to voicemail. Is everything okay?" The laugh that escaped me sounded slightly hysterical even to my own ears.

"No, everything's not okay, Daniel! I just. I can't do this anymore. I can't handle everything on my own with you gone for so long. It's just too much!" I felt the tears start to run down my face all over again.

"I understand, babe," he pleaded gently. "I know it's been so hard with mom's injuries and recovery taking longer than expected. I left you on your own to manage the home front, and I feel torn about it every day. But, honey, her doctor finally gave the all-clear today for me to bring her home."

My breath caught in my throat. "So, you're coming home for good, then?" Daniel hesitated. "Well, not quite yet." Daniel let out a deep breath. "Honey, I want to come back home. I miss all of you, especially you. But, if I'm to get back, Mom will have to move in with us for a while during the transition. Her mobility is still limited. This will be just until she finishes physical therapy.

I'm so sorry to ask this of you right now, but I can't leave her alone, and I really need to get back to all of you." I slumped down onto the couch in the living room, my eyes on the overpacked suitcases. All strength and manic energy drained from my body.

Of course, our lives couldn't simply go back to normal just because Daniel was returning home. There was always just one more sacrifice needed from me. When I stayed silent, Daniel continued earnestly, "I know it's so much, and it is all on your shoulders. This is more than I have the right to ask of you. But if we could figure out a way to move Mom in, even temporarily, I swear I'll make it up to you, Rachel. Please don't give up on me, on us. You mean everything to me."

His words pierced my heart. I knew, logically, that he was right, and it wasn't his fault either. I was just so emotionally and physically exhausted that I was unable to cope with any more changes or demands. And, I knew if Lucia moved in, I'd have to help with her care. This was in addition to the pressure of taking care of three children.

Did I have a choice, other than to accept his mother, Lucia, into our already strained home situation? I had to be strong for just a little while longer. Daniel needed me to be.

Swallowing the resentment burning sourly in my throat, I whispered at last, "Okay. We'll find a way to make it work."

"Thank you. Thank you so much, Rachel," Daniel said, relief flooding his voice. "I know this isn't easy, but I promise we'll get through this."

I sighed, running a hand through my hair. "I guess; just let me know when your flight gets in. The kids will be excited to see you." "We're booked on a non-stop flight. We should be there around eight if all goes smoothly," he replied.

"Today?" I heard Daniel's deep laughter on the end of the phone. God, but I loved that honey-smooth laugh. I felt my heart melt a little. "Sure. I need to finish up a few things here, but I'll see you real soon, babe."

Slowly, I carried the suitcases and my phone back into the bedroom. I sat on the bed, thinking. I heard the kids burst loudly through the front door, back from school. Their carefree chatter usually brought a smile to my heart, but today it signified that my window had been shut. I had waited too long to leave, and now it was too late.

"The kids are back, I gotta go." "Alright, babe. Give them a kiss for me. Love you, hon." I paused, thinking. I did love Daniel. I always would. "I lo-," I started. But before I could finish the words, there was silence from the other end.

I sat still for some moments, trying to make sense of where I was emotionally a few minutes ago, and where I'd suddenly been catapulted to by Daniel's call.

A soft but confident knock brought me to the present. "Y-", I cleared my throat, and forced my voice to be louder. "Yes?" Sandra, Daniel's oldest, pushed the bedroom door open, peeping in. "Hi, Rachel. We're back. Are there any snacks?"

I forced brightness into my tone. "Hi, honey. I'm sorry. I got caught up in something else. There's apples and carrots in the fridge. Help your brother and sister fix plates, please." "Okay." I could hear the disappointment in her voice.

I'm sure she thought I didn't care about her. As her footsteps retreated down the hall, I rose slowly from the bed and wandered over to Daniel's desk. Feeling nostalgic, I pulled the bottom cabinet open, looking for our wedding pictures.

I started to pull them out, when I saw a couple of letters beside them. The return address was Lucia's. When had Daniel received these letters from his mom, and why didn't he tell me about them?

I sank into the chair and began reading Lucia's elegant cursive script, dated from around the time of our wedding. As the words leapt out from the page, a knot formed in my stomach.

She was reminding Daniel how close they had always been, even during his first marriage. Lucia had wanted them to honor certain family wedding traditions at our wedding, the way they had the first time.

My insisting otherwise had caused tension between us. "I just hope you aren't making a mistake marrying Rachel, and you won't decide to choose her over your own mother," Lucia had written. "You deserve a wife who puts you and your family first."

I remembered our heated arguments over wedding plans. Lucia kept inserting her opinions and traditions until I'd felt no ownership of my own ceremony. In the end I'd capitulated on most things, just to keep some semblance of peace.

Daniel had supported me, but clearly Lucia hadn't let any of it go. My pulse pounded in my ears. How were we supposed to live together if she thought I wasn't good enough for her son? I felt sick imagining the criticisms and drama to come.

Maybe leaving was still the right choice. I went downstairs to start an early dinner for the kids and get the house ready for Daniel and his mother. A couple of hours later, Amy and Michael chattered with infectious enthusiasm all through dinner about daddy coming home.

My daughter was the petite mirror image of me. She had dark curls framing a heart-shaped face, which was currently alight with joy. Michael, a year younger but growing like a weed, had Daniel's warm brown eyes that crinkled the exact same way when he smiled. "Is Daddy going to sleep in your room when he gets back, or can he have a slumber party in my room?" Amy asked around a mouthful of spaghetti.

I smoothed a hand over her hair, swallowing past the lump in my throat. "We'll see, sweetie. Daddy will be pretty tired from taking care of Grandma."

Sandra was more subdued. Her waist-length mink brown hair curtained her face as she silently twirled noodles on her fork. So, Nana's going to stay with us for a while, once she and Dad get back later tonight," I said slowly, watching their reactions. "That means some adjustments for all of us."

Sandra lifted her head at last, chewing her full bottom lip. Her angelic blue eyes, a replica of her late mother's, were full of uncertainty. "We'll figure it out, honey," I hastened to reassure her with a smile I didn't quite feel. I know change can be difficult, but it'll be alright." She just nodded silently and returned her gaze to her plate.

My heart ached for my sensitive stepdaughter. She had lost her own mom at a young age and gone through so much upheaval already in her short life. Now we were asking her to disrupt her safe little world yet again.

Later, as I cleaned up, I felt the familiar wave of exhaustion and self-doubt rise again, threatening to crash over me. I fought to keep my turmoil hidden, plastering on a cheerful smile. With Lucia arriving imminently, I had to hold us together no matter my private fears.

Tonight, I would pray for strength and wisdom to navigate the choppy waters still ahead.

Dear God, please help our family. Please let us work through this challenge together.

I was a bundle of nerves as I waited by the front window for the sight of the taxi bringing Daniel and Lucia back. When it finally pulled into the driveway, I hurried out onto the front steps just as he was helping his mother carefully out of the passenger seat. Before I knew it, strong familiar arms were wrapped tight around me. As I sank into Daniel's embrace, breathing in his soothing scent, all the fear and tension of the past lonely weeks seemed to drain away.

Unexpected tears spilled down my cheeks. "Shhh; I'm here now babe," Daniel murmured, cradling the back of my head. I just clung to him, unable to form words around the sudden release of emotions. Over his shoulder, I glimpsed Lucia standing by the car with one hand gripping her cane. She looked so much older and frailer than the last time I'd seen her. Blinking back my tears, I pulled gently out of Daniel's arms as the screen door crashed open.

Amy and Michael quickly hurtled past, shouting "Daddy!" They grabbed onto his legs like exuberant puppies. "There are my darlings!" Daniel picked Michael up and held him in a tight hug, kissing him on his face, before he sat him down and did the same for Amy. Next, they hugged Lucia, and she ruffled their hair, asking them how they were. A watery chuckle escaped my throat at their unrestrained enthusiasm.

Sandra had appeared, also, but hung back on the steps as everyone exchanged excited greetings and hugs. Daniel held Sandra longer than he'd held onto everyone else, and I watched them together. He stroked her hair; she looked up at him, her eyes filled with love. For the first time in a long time, Sandra had a wide smile on her face.

Lucia's lined face softened slightly as she beheld her son's children clustered around him after the long separation. I pasted on a polite smile. "It's good to see you again, Lucia. Let's go in so you can get settled in. It's a bit windy out here." Daniel squeezed my shoulder gently before turning to gather luggage and help his children inside, their chattering voices fading down the hall.

Lucia studied me for a long moment with her piercing dark eyes. At last, she inclined her head. "That would be welcome, Rachel. It has been a difficult journey for these old bones." I led the way inside, every nerve ending jittery having her here under my roof at last. This was really happening, whether I felt ready or not. There was so much complicated history here. I had tried so hard to be good enough in her estimation, but nothing ever seemed sufficient for Daniel's formidable mother.

We were virtual strangers bound by familial ties and mutual love for Daniel. Could bygones be bygones? Or was more heartache inevitable? Only time would tell if this overcrowded house could hold our fractured relationships as well.

I opened the door to guest bedroom, on the second floor. I stepped inside, allowing room for her to come in. "This will be your room, Lucia." I'd wanted her to have this room, for the early morning sun that filtered in, bathing the room with its warmth and beauty. I smiled, expecting her joy when she saw the blue, yellow and white decor. Lucia stepped in and looked around the room. The smile gradually faded when I saw her frown.

Just then Daniel brought in his mother's suitcases. Lucia turned to me, "This won't do, dear. I need to be on the ground floor at my age," she said in a clipped tone. "Those stairs are too risky. We'll have to move some things around." I pressed my lips together, irked at her instant demand. "The only bedroom on the main floor is mine and Daniel's. The kids' rooms are all upstairs, too."

She waved a dismissive hand. "Then I'll take the den off the kitchen. Just have Daniel move the desk and television elsewhere. The sofa pulls out into a bed, yes?" Without waiting for my assent, Lucia grasped her cane and shuffled down the stairs to assess the den space, murmuring about needing her cross-stitching chair and reading lamp.

Daniel and I exchanged looks. Mine was stormy; his pleaded with me. *Uh, oh. This is going to be worse than I thought!*

With a frustrated sigh, I followed slowly, trying to ignore the simmering annoyance at her presumption. She thought she could dictate whatever changes she wished. This was in my home, too, even if it was her son's house.

When I entered the den, Lucia was already rearranging the chairs. "I told Daniel over and over that I do not need to be moving in with you all," she grumbled. "Just because I had some trouble getting around is no reason to disrupt everyone else's life. "I may not be a spring chicken anymore, but there's nothing wrong with my mind or disposition," Lucia said. "I just need some help until this blasted back heals fully."

Despite her prickly nature, I had to admire Lucia's fierce independence and pride. I knew Daniel likely pressured her into staying with us for her safety. She was making concessions, too. Taking a deep breath, I moved forward to squeeze her shoulder gently. "Why don't I make us some tea while Daniel brings your things in?" "That would be lovely. Thank you, Rachel," she replied with a small nod, the hard lines on her face softened, faintly.

I sensed our truce was tentative but vital for weathering the transition ahead.

But the night was about to take a turn for the worse.

Before I went to make tea, I decided to find Daniel first. I pushed the door to our bedroom open, and found Daniel sitting by my packed suitcases, reading the note I'd left him saying goodbye.

Friction and Reflection

Daniel

I sank down on the bed, stunned by the words scrawled in Rachel's familiar looping script. *She had been planning to leave me, take Amy and disappear into the night. I mean really leave me. Was it for good?*

Anger and hurt roiled my chest. *How could she do this, abandon our family when I needed her the most?*

I thought we were stronger than this. Just then, Rachel appeared in the doorway. She froze when she saw the note in my hands. Her face paled and she opened her mouth, but no words came out.

"You were just going to go, just like that?" My voice came out harsher than I intended, giving in to my swirling emotions. "Without talking to me first, telling me how you felt?"

Rachel wrapped her arms around herself, not meeting my gaze. "I... things have just been so hard, Daniel," she whispered. "Doing everything on my own. I was at my breaking point."

"You should've told me!" I rose and paced, raking a hand through my hair. "God, Rachel, if I'd had any idea you were struggling this much, of course, I would've come home sooner."

"Would you have?" She finally met my eyes, hers shining with tears. "Or would you have kept focusing only on your mom's needs and giving me one excuse after another for staying away longer?" I flinched. "That's not fair. She's my mother; she needed me."

"And I'm your wife!" Rachel cried. "I and the kids needed you, too, but it felt like we didn't matter. It felt like we just had to deal with it all alone." Her words pierced my heart. I took three deep breaths and moved forward, grasping her hands gently in mine. "Rachel, I'm so sorry I made you feel that way. Of course, you and our children are my first priority. I should've been here for you all."

She took a shuddering breath. "No, I shouldn't have just assumed you'd know how I was feeling. I need to open up instead of letting things build up like this. Can you forgive me?" I pulled her close, my anger already dissipating. "Of course, if you can forgive me for being blind to your needs. No more secrets, okay? We're in this together." I brushed a soft kiss over her hair as she nestled into my embrace. For better or worse, we would weather every storm as one from here forward. I leaned in and gave her a gentle kiss on her lips. "Let's go make some tea for Mom." We managed to have tea in peace. Not wanting to tempt the truce, I kissed Mom afterwards. Then, I told her that Rachel and I wanted to get rest.

I awoke to the sound of cartoons blaring from the living room TV, mingling with giggles and shouts from the kids.

Glancing at the clock, I stifled a groan. It was barely 7 AM and the house was already a zoo.

Padding out to the kitchen in my pajamas, I found Amy sitting on the counter while Lucia tried navigating around her small swinging legs to cook breakfast.

Michael was dumping Legos out onto the floor, ignoring Lucia's admonishments.

"Who wants chocolate chip pancakes?" I announced over the din, lifting Amy down. She and Michael cheered while Sandra remained glued to the TV.

"You don't need to do that; I'm cooking just fine," Lucia said crisply, taking bowls out of my hands. I bit back a retort, moving to start a pot of coffee instead.

Ever since Lucia moved in last week, she had taken over the kitchen as her domain. I knew she was trying to make herself useful, but Rachel felt displaced from her own space.

Speaking of the devil, Rachel shuffled in. Her brown hair was adorably mussed from sleep. Before I could give her a good morning kiss,

Michael came barreling over, knocking into her legs. "Oof, walk please, buddy!" Rachel said, grabbing the counter for balance.

But Michael had already dashed away again, yelling "Beep. Beep. Coming through!" I winced as Rachel's face clouded with irritation. She avoided my attempt to massage her shoulders, muttering "I need to get ready," before escaping back to our room.

Over breakfast, I noticed Sandra was barely eating, just pushing her pancakes around listlessly. "Everything okay, kiddo?" I asked. She glanced up and nodded; her large blue eyes were solemn. My sweet girl was so sensitive. I will make a mental note to spend one-on-one time with her, later. Just then Amy spilled her juice. Michael started banging his fork loudly, and Lucia berated them to, "act civilized." I dragged a hand down my face, feeling a headache coming on.

How were we going to adjust to these chaotic new dynamics? For my family's sake, we had to find a balance soon before tensions boiled over. "Alright kids, everyone into the living room."

I managed to corral the kids and lead them away, giving the kitchen a brief respite. But soon I heard raised voices drifting in. Heading back, I found Lucia and Rachel standing on opposite sides of the kitchen island, both flushed. A broken bowl lay at Rachel's feet. "I was just trying to help wash up from breakfast, dear," Lucia said in an overly patient tone. Rachel crossed her arms tightly. "Well, I had a system going already until you pushed in and took over half the counter. You made me drop that bowl."

"It was an accident; there is no need for histrionics," Lucia huffed. I cleared my throat before the simmering tension erupted further. "Hey, it's getting a bit busy for all of us to be washing up at the same time. Lucia, why don't I help you tidy your room while Rachel finishes up in here?"

Lucia opened her mouth like she wanted to argue, then seemed to reconsider when she saw my pleading look. "Fine. I do have clothes that need folding." As we left, I squeezed Rachel's shoulder in solidarity. I knew having her space overrun was grating on her nerves.

We were out of sync, but we needed to find our rhythm as a newly blended household. "With patience and adaptability, we would get there.

Next, I heard raised voices in the family room. Amy and Sandra were arguing about whose turn it was to choose the TV show. I chose the TV show; they settled down to watch. Each was just happy that the other didn't win. As I left them in reluctant truce, I shook my head tiredly. Patience was key, but it seemed to be in short supply these days. The day passed, more or less normally.

Rachel and I needed to carve out couple-time soon, before the constant balancing acts pushed us to the brink. For now, quieting this latest skirmish would have to be enough.

Speaking of Rachel, where was she? I found her sitting alone in the dark living room with a cup of tea. She started when I flipped on the light. "Oh, hey," she said dully, not meeting my eyes. I sat down and rubbed her knee. "Long day, huh?" She let out a mirthless laugh. "Nowadays? That's putting it mildly. I finally got Michael to sleep after three stories, only for the girls to start shrieking at each other over closet space or something. Then your mom decided to start vacuuming her room right as I was drifting off."

I winced. "I'm sorry. I should've asked her to wait until morning." Rachel turned to me with glistening eyes. "Do you think we made a mistake? Agreeing to move your mom in when we were barely holding it together before?" My heart ached at seeing her so despondent.

I drew her into my arms, stroking her hair as she laid her head on my shoulder. "I know things are chaotic right now, but it's just an adjustment period. We knew going in it wouldn't be easy."

She sighed heavily. "I just wonder sometimes. Was it selfish of me to want you home instead of caring for your mom? I feel like such a failure." "You are not a failure," I said fiercely, tilting her chin up to meet her defeated gaze. "You're the strongest woman I know, and an amazing mother. This is just a season, and we'll get through it together."

Rachel managed a small smile, then snuggled into me. The path ahead remained uncertain, but we would walk it as a united front, wherever it led.

The next morning, I came out to find Lucia sitting alone at the kitchen table, staring out the window with a melancholy air. "Everything okay, Mom?" I asked, squeezing her shoulder. She patted my hand absently. "Oh yes, just these old bones creaking. Don't mind me."

But over the next few days, she grew more subdued. She stopped trying to take over the kitchen, avoided getting underfoot, and spent her time shut away in her room. Thankfully, she had finally agreed to move into the guest room upstairs, and at least my mind was at ease that she was more comfortable.

Meanwhile, Rachel became more on edge as she struggled to manage the kids and household solo, again. I was back at the office. One evening, after the kids were in bed, I checked on Lucia. She was sitting upright in her bed, face drawn. "What's really going on, Mom? Talk to me," I prodded gently. She sighed, eyes downcast. "I just feel like I'm in the way here. You both have your hands full with the little ones, and I'm only adding to Rachel's burden."

I squeezed her hand. "Hey, you're not a burden; we want you here. This is just an adjustment period. Rachel and I need to figure out how to better support each other so you don't feel caught in the middle."

Lucia nodded but still seemed troubled. I resolved to talk to Rachel about addressing the lingering tensions head-on. United, we could make this unusual living situation work for all. I sat alone late into the night, thoughts churning endlessly. Ever since my talk with mom, I'd been wrestling with how to ease the tensions that enveloped our home. On one hand, I wanted to be fully present for Rachel and the kids. I wanted to make up for lost time and support them during this chaotic transition. They deserved my undivided attention. But at the same time, I couldn't neglect Mom's needs either, now that her mobility was limited. I owed her so much - she had practically raised me solo after Dad passed, working tirelessly to provide while still being an affectionate, involved parent.

Abandoning her now, even temporarily, went against everything she had taught me about duty and sacrifice. These competing pulls left me paralyzed, afraid to act in case I upset one side's delicate balance. It seemed I couldn't be an ideal husband or perfect son while we were all under the same roof. Someone's needs would inevitably be unmet.

My gaze fell on our old family photo albums lining the bookshelf. I pulled out a faded blue one embossed "Our Memories" in curling gold script. Flipping slowly through sun-dappled snapshots of easier times, bittersweet nostalgia swelled in my chest.

Here we were camping as a young family. I couldn't have been more than five, proudly holding up the fish I'd caught. Mom hugged me, laughing. Another page showed my parents dancing at their anniversary party, gazes locked adoringly. Then, there was a picture of mom and I baking Christmas cookies. Flour was smudged everywhere, but we were both grinning ear to ear.

How had we drifted so far from that unbridled joy and closeness? When did the unchecked busyness and tangled obligations of life draw up suffocating walls between us? We were still the same people inside who once loved each other so openly. Was restoring that connection still possible?

I lingered over a photo of Rachel kissing Amy. The tenderness emanating from her face in that fragile moment pierced my heart. Then there was a photo of all five of us. We'd gone to the carnival that day. Everyone had a bright, happy expression on their faces, and we looked like the perfect family. We were the type nothing could pull down. We had built a family together. That still had to count for something. Closing the album, I knelt and bowed my head. *"Lord, please help me reunite my family again,"* I prayed fervently. *"Mend the hurt, soothe the tensions robbing our home of peace. Guide me to meet their needs while still honoring my marriage vows. Grant us all patience and grace to see each other with loving eyes once more.*

Help me lead us through this wilderness back to joy again. In Jesus' name. Amen."

A blanket of calm slowly enveloped me, easing the clenched strain within my spirit. With faith and open hearts willing to sacrifice for one another, we could rebuild the bonds time had worn thin. Tomorrow was a new day. I would begin again, and keep beginning, until we found our way.

A Hidden Blessing Amidst Chaos

Rachel

I watched Michael smash his food around his plate, my head pounding. "Please just take three more bites, then you can be done." He whined and pushed the plate away. Any other day I would've calmly encouraged him, but today my fraying patience snapped. "Just eat it!" I yelled, slamming my hand on the table.

Michael's lip quivered. I took a deep breath, softening my tone. "I'm sorry honey, Mommy's just not feeling well." Lucia gave me a probing look as she took Michael's plate to the sink. I avoided her eyes, knowing I'd been irritable and on edge for weeks now. I chalked it up to the never-ending chaos since she moved in. But deep down, I knew something more was going on. The exhaustion plaguing me, the nausea, the fact that I was late for the third month in a row now.

Somewhere, in my gut, I already suspected. But I pushed that inkling down, not ready to confront its implications. After getting the kids to sleep that night, I headed out alone to the grocery store. In the feminine hygiene aisle, my hands shook slightly as I grabbed a pregnancy test, along with tampons. Surely the test would be negative, and this nagging worry would go away.

But an hour later, as I sat on the closed toilet lid staring at the two pink lines, all my denials fell away. I was pregnant. We were having another baby, when we already had no time or energy for the three we had. Daniel and I were still learning to communicate again after the distance between us. Our relationship felt too fragile for the upheaval of a new life. And where would we even put the nursery with Lucia occupying the guest room?

As I lay sleepless that night, scenes of all the ways this could further destabilize our precarious household played through my mind like a film reel. We had just regained a semblance of balance. Now, it would likely be lost again, washed away by a rogue wave of change we hadn't seen coming.

Morning came; yet rest remained elusive. My mind spun with logistics - how would we afford another baby when I had no job? Could Daniel take on more clients? Maybe we could convert the garage to a small nursery. I had so many questions but not one reassuring answer. I shuffled to the bathroom, catching a glimpse of my pallid face in the mirror. The dark circles under my eyes stood out starkly, evidence of the anxiety churning within. I splashed cold water on my skin, willing myself to keep up appearances just a little longer.

In the kitchen, I stared blankly at the chore chart on the fridge, yesterday's tensions replaying. Lucia and I had argued over her loading the dishwasher wrong, while the kids bickered loudly. Just another day in our crowded chaos. Now another small being would join the fray. My hands drifted absently over my still-flat stomach under my baggy sweatshirt. A new life was growing there, fragile and dependent solely on me. Could I protect and nurture it adequately? Doubt clouded my thoughts, threatening to swallow me whole.

Just then, Daniel suddenly entered, his presence momentarily lifting the heavy mood. "Morning," he said briskly, leaning in to plant a quick kiss on my forehead. His routine was always the same, brief and hurried. "Morning," I replied, forcing a small smile. I needed him today.

"Daniel, do you —" "I'm late already, honey" he cut in, grabbing his keys from the counter. "Can it wait until tonight?" I hesitated, the words I needed to say stuck in my throat. "It's just" I forced a smile. "... yeah, sure. We can talk later. Have a good day..."

He paused at the door, his expression softening for a moment. "We'll figure it out, you know? We always do. I gotta run. Love you." And just like that, he was gone. His truck rumbled down the road, leaving me alone with my mounting fears and unanswered questions.

I watched through the window, tears blurring my vision, wishing for once he could stay and help me shoulder these burdens. But this was our reality. His absences loomed large when he went to work. Even when he was home, he was busy juggling his roles as father, son and husband. It seemed as if I was at the bottom of the priority list though.

I was always left trying to cope alone. Even with the kids at school, and Lucia taking a nap in her room, by afternoon the confines of my home felt increasingly suffocating. I grabbed my purse and escaped to one haven I knew. This was the flower-lined path leading to the rectory. The vibrant multi-colored blooms always seemed to offer a silent understanding of my inner turmoil.

As I sat among the flowers, lost in thought, the pastor unexpectedly emerged from the rectory. His appearance was a gentle reminder of the many times his wise counsel had aided so many. I rarely sought him out, due to my reserved nature. "Ah, Rachel, dear child, what brings you here? The Spring blooms?" he asked, his voice a calm presence in my stormy thoughts.

Startled, I managed a weak smile. "Yes. The flowers are lovely. And also, just... seeking some peace, pastor." He nodded knowingly and gestured towards the church. "Sometimes peace is found in sharing burdens. Come, let's talk inside." Reluctantly, I followed him, and we moved to his modest office.

I sank into the familiar worn wooden chair across from him. His presence, like a steady anchor, encouraged me to open up. "Pastor, it's just... everything feels too much," I began, my voice trembling. "Daniel is always busy, and now, I'm expecting a baby. With another child on the way, I don't know how to cope."

Pastor listened, his weathered hands resting calmly in his lap. "Life's trials often seem insurmountable, but remember, you're not alone in this journey." His words encouraged me, and I poured out my heart. I told him about the growing isolation, the strain in my marriage, the relentless chaos with Lucia, and the fear of how this pregnancy might unbalance our already precarious life.

"Each challenge," he said softly, "is also an opportunity for growth, for strength. How can you turn this into a positive path forward?" I paused, considering his words. " I don't know, Pastor. I'm just so scared." "Trust in yourself," he encouraged. "And remember, support can come from unexpected places. Have you discussed these fears with Daniel?"

I shook my head. "He's always so busy, and I don't want to burden him more." "Sometimes," Pastor advised, "sharing a burden can lighten it. Open up to Daniel; work together. I'm sure you'll find strength in each other."

As our conversation drew to a close, the knot of anxiety in my chest had loosened slightly. Pastor's words had offered a glimmer of hope, a reminder that I wasn't as alone as I felt.

Stepping out of the rectory, I felt a renewed sense of resolve to face the challenges ahead. Feeling better after my talk with our pastor, I decided to make Daniel's favorite pot roast to soften the blow of my news. It was inevitable that I would tell him about the baby. The earlier I did it, the better we'd both adjust to our new reality.

But when I heard his truck pull up, my nerves skyrocketed. The slamming of the truck door made me jump, and before I could gather myself, the front door swung violently open. "Rachel?" Daniel's voice rang out sharply. He stormed into the kitchen; jaw tight. I blinked in surprise. "You're home early. Is everything okay?" "I got a call from June; said she saw you coming out of the rectory today." "Yes, I wanted to see-" Daniel cut me off. "Alone." My heart sank as understanding dawned. June was the neighborhood gossip.

"Daniel, I know how it could have looked," I began carefully. "But I just needed some guidance about everything going on here."

"So, you couldn't come to me?" Daniel crossed his arms. "Had to talk to another man behind my back?" Stung, I retorted, "You're never here to talk to! I didn't want to bother you at work over this. Even when I tried to talk, you told me it could wait."

Daniel raked a hand through his hair in frustration. "Don't you get it, Rachel? Nothing is more important than you and our family. You should've told me the moment you started struggling, not bottled it up then ran to the pastor!"

The accusation in his tone made my hackles rise. "Oh, so this is all my fault? I've been drowning for weeks trying to hold us together solo. But sure, I should've magically known you'd want to talk when you got back from work, even after you told me in the morning to wait!

I bet if it was your mother who wanted something, you wouldn't have told her to wait," I added, with a murmur. "Don't bring my mother into this! I told you I had no choice."

We stood toe to toe, chests heaving. All the tensions simmering below the surface had ruptured like a volcano. Finally, Daniel broke the ringing silence, his voice hoarse. "Enough. I refuse to be angry with you. Can we please talk openly?"

I sighed, the fight seeping from my bones as quickly as it came. We moved to the couch, both wrapping our arms around ourselves defensively. Haltingly, I whispered, "You're right. I should have come to you first. But things have felt so broken between us lately, I didn't know how."

Daniel's face softened with regret. "I never meant to be so distant, Rachel. I thought focusing on work and Mom was the right thing. Once again, I neglected you, and I'm so sorry."

I took a deep shuddering breath as we broke apart from a reconciliatory embrace. It was now or never. "Daniel, there's something else I need to tell you." My hands twisted together nervously in my lap. He grasped my fidgeting fingers in his strong ones. "Hey, whatever it is, we'll figure it out together. I'm here now."

I nodded, blinking back a fresh wave of tears. "I'm pregnant."

Daniel's eyes widened in shock, mouth falling open. For a few breathless moments, only the ticking of the wall clock filled the heavy silence. Finally, he choked out, "Pregnant? But how? We've been so careful."

My laugh held a tinge of hysteria. "Well, it must have happened that weekend after your mom first moved in. We weren't as careful as usual given our happy reunion."

Daniel dragged a hand down his face, leaning forward with elbows on knees. "Rachel, what are we going to do? This is the absolute worst timing; we already have no space or privacy!" Panic clawed at my throat as I heard him voice my own fears out loud. I started rambling, hands twisting the hem of my shirt. "I don't know; we'll have to make the garage into a nursery, somehow.

We'll hope you can pick up more clients. I can try to work from home." "Whoa, whoa, slow down," Daniel interrupted, grasping my restless hands again. "We'll figure all that out later. Let's just take a breath first."

I yanked my hands away, fresh anger rising to the surface. "Take a breath? I've already been freaking out about this all day on my own! You don't get to swoop in with platitudes, when I'm the one who has to grow a human being in the midst of this circus!"

Daniel held up his palms in a placating gesture. "You're right honey; I'm still processing this. But getting worked up won't help. We have to trust that God will provide a way even if we can't see it yet." I crossed my arms, glare sharpening. "Oh, so I should just pray my worries away, huh? Don't be naive Daniel, it takes more than faith to raise a baby!" He sighed, running a hand through his hair. "Our faith is being tested; that's all.

Another child is a blessing we can't yet fully grasp. But together, leaning on God's help, we'll find a way. Please don't lose hope Rachel." As Daniel's earnest words sank in, the fight slowly left my body. He was right. Spiraling into fear wouldn't change what was coming. And hadn't we overcome impossible odds before?

Resting my hand over my still flat stomach, I allowed a spark of excitement to flicker amidst the uncertainty. With courage and trust, we would navigate this unexpected gift one step at a time. As we opened up fully, tears and apologies flowed freely.

We talked more than we had since Daniel returned. And together, we started slowly trying to figure out solutions. We talked about what we could do so the baby could have a room. We wondered if there was any way we could increase our income. Most importantly, we promised to make our relationship the bedrock going forward, no matter what storms raged outside. Though fragile and scarred, with care, our love could be made new.

Dreaming of Harmony

Daniel

Rachel and I stayed seated at the kitchen island, hands clasped, as we heard the kids burst through the front door.

Their bright voices carried down the hall, mingling with the shuffle of Lucia's slow gait behind them.

I pressed a quick kiss to Rachel's temple as she offered me a tremulous, brave smile. It was time to share our news and face the family's reaction together.

"Hey guys, how about we eat outside tonight?" I called. "It's too nice out not to enjoy our meal by the pool."

Amidst the excited cheers, Lucia narrowed her eyes at me.

"Daniel, you know I prefer to eat properly at the dining table."

But I just smiled, buzzing with nervous energy. "It's not too cold yet, Mom. Come on, it'll be an adventure. Besides the change will do you good!"

Soon we had paper plates and plastic cutlery set up on the patio tables, while Lucia arranged serving dishes of the pot roast and sides we had cooked earlier.

Cicadas droned in the trees surrounding the backyard as the setting sun cast a warm, orange glow.

Once everyone was settled with food, I caught Rachel's eye and nodded. Clearing my throat, I began a little awkwardly, "So, Rachel and I have some exciting news to share with you all. Our family is oing to grow soon."

"A new puppy?" Amy shrieked. Michael's face lit up, too.

"Yay! A puppy."

I chuckled. "No sweetie, even better than a puppy. You're going to have a new baby brother or sister!" Gasps rang out around the table. Lucia froze, fork halfway to her mouth.

The kids at once began clamoring with questions on top of each other. "When will the baby get here?" "Can it sleep in my room?"

Only Sandra was silent. She was chewing her lip. I reached over to squeeze her hand. "I know it's a surprise, but isn't a new baby exciting, too?" She gave a small smile that didn't quite reach her eyes. "Yes. But, where will the baby even stay? Our house is already so full of all of us."

I exchanged a glance with Rachel, seeing my own veiled concerns reflected on her face. But I kept my tone confident as I replied, "We'll figure all that out soon, don't you worry! A new life is always a blessing."

Sandra just nodded, unconvinced, and returned to pushing her food around. I ruffled her hair, leaning forward to kiss the top of her head. My heart ached for my sensitive daughter, who craved stability and was now being asked to weather yet more upheaval.

But I gazed around the table at my family, tired Rachel, wary Lucia, and the excited younger kids. I knew this child knitting itself to life in Rachel's womb belonged with us, no matter how uncertain I felt. We would make room at the inn for this miracle, even when the lodging seemed full already.

With faith in the Author of Life, our story would unfold exactly as it should. I raised my glass of fruit punch, waiting for the excited chatter to die down. "I know there are a lot of uncertainties right now, but I have faith that we'll figure everything out, together. God brought this child to us for a reason. It may feel scary facing the unknown, but we have to trust that He'll guide us through it."

Rachel gave my hand a grateful squeeze under the table. I could see the fear in her eyes lessening just a fraction at my words. "Yeah, God's got this!" piped up Michael through a mouthful of potatoes.

We all chuckled at my exuberant son. Swallowing his bite, he continued innocently, "We don't gotta worry, God is SOOO big that our problem will be teeny tiny to Him!" He held his thumb and pointer finger half an inch apart to show his idea. Laughter rippled around the table at his simple proclamation of faith. Lucia shook her head with a reluctant smile while Rachel smoothed a hand over Michael's curls. Even stoic Sandra seemed to sit a little lighter.

The atmosphere turned festive again as we passed dishes and filled plates for seconds. Conversation ebbed and flowed. Amy was peppering Rachel with questions about the baby. Lucia was musing about converting the office into a nursery. Michael entertained us with silly jokes.

Under the glow of patio lights, the uncertainty of tomorrow faded for a few treasured hours. We were just a family breaking bread on a mild summer night. Our hearts were full of love and hope. Whatever storms lay ahead, we would weather them as one, with generosity, understanding, and trust that there was a purpose beyond what we could yet see.

Faith would light our way, step by step, even through the darkest nights. That night after dinner, I knelt by the bed as had become my habit. Bowing my head, I prayed fervently, *"Lord, please show me how to unify my divided house. Guide my steps to restore peace and joy again to these relationships so worn thin. Open my eyes to see a solution to our cramped quarters."*

I prayed with the same fervency the next night, and the one after that. Then on the third night, I drifted off still wrestling with half-formed ideas of converting the garage or attic into a livable space. As I slipped into dreaming, a vision began to unfold. I saw Lucia's cozy bungalow, nestled on a quiet side street. She was placing a "For Sale" sign in the front yard. The scene shifted to our house, where construction workers were building a beautiful expanded addition that blended seamlessly with the original structure. Inside, Lucia smiled contentedly in a private suite connected to the rest of the home. I awoke with sunlight streaming through the curtains, the details of the dream playing over my mind.

Could this have been...a vision from the Lord? The elegance and simplicity of the solution struck me with sudden clarity. Of course, if mom sold her house, we could use the money to build her an addition here so she wouldn't have to fully depend on us but could remain close!

My heart quickened with anticipation tinged by uncertainty. *How would Rachel react to this proposal? It would mean Mom would be living with us for the rest of her life. And would Mom want to leave her home of thirty years? But hadn't I prayed for God's guidance in this? I had to trust His wisdom over my doubts.*

Filled with nervous energy, I rose and dressed quickly. It was time to share the idea budding within me. This could lead our family into restored harmony. We just needed faith to walk the path that was illuminated before us, taking one step at a time.

At breakfast, I could barely hold my excitement. I wanted to share the idea inspired by my dream. As the last bites of pancakes were eaten, I cleared my throat. "So, I've been thinking and praying a lot about our limited space with a new baby on the way," I began. "Last night, I had this dream. Mom was able to sell her house and use that money to build an addition here. She would have her own suite. We could also build an extra room for the baby. This could solve many of our problems!"

I gazed around expectantly at the surprised faces. Lucia was the first to speak, shaking her head in dismissal. "Oh Daniel, you and your wild ideas. I can't just sell my home of 30 years on a whim!" "But, Mom, it's perfect!" I argued. "You'd have your privacy but stay close. And we'd get desperately needed room." She sighed. "It's a lovely thought dear, but where would I even go during construction?"

I faltered, not having considered that complication. Deciding to regroup, I turned to Rachel who was staring silently down at her lap. "What do you think, hon? Could this work?" Her shoulders tensed almost imperceptibly before she flashed a bright, placating smile. "Well, like Lucia said, it's a sweet idea in theory," she trailed off diplomatically.

I felt a twinge of hurt at her lack of enthusiasm. I'd half expected it, but I thought she'd at least give the whole thing a chance. But before I could probe further, Amy piped up. "Nana Lucia can live in my dollhouse! It's soooo big." We all chuckled at the mental image. Only Michael shared my untempered excitement, grinning up at me. "I like your dream, Daddy! The baby can stay in my room." Rachel smoothed his hair affectionately. "That's very sweet of you to offer Michael, but the baby will need their own space."

I didn't miss the anxiety lurking beneath her smile. She must be picturing endless nights trying to soothe a fussy newborn 32 without privacy. This wasn't exactly the leap of faith I'd been expecting my dream proposal to inspire. Trying to rekindle momentum, I said gently, "It's just a thought for now. But will you all at least pray and reflect if this could be the right move for our family?"

Lucia and Rachel exchanged a skeptical look but eventually assented. I planted the seed. Now, I just had to keep faith that it would grow. I would nurture it patiently. With God's help, my dream could pave the way to unity and harmony again, under one roof. After breakfast, I pulled Rachel aside while Lucia helped clean up. "Hey, you were pretty quiet about my idea earlier. What are your hesitations?" I asked.

Rachel wrapped her arms around herself protectively. "I just don't know if permanently combining households is the best solution for us right now. What if we end up feeling suffocated?" I tilted my head. "Suffocated how?"

She sighed, her gaze not meeting my eyes. "I already feel like I've lost myself trying to be everything to everyone. If your mom officially lives here, it may get worse with her opinions on raising kids and everything." I stepped closer, nudging her chin up gently so our eyes met. "Rachel, I would never want you to feel that way. If we do this, we'll set boundaries to protect our autonomy as parents." "It's not that simple." she whispered.

My heart sank as I began to understand her deeper fears. An addition meant final acceptance of Lucia's permanent presence. This would reshape the contours of our home and family life. Drawing Rachel close, I murmured, "This is our choice, our home. No matter what changes, I will always put you and our kids first. Please keep an open mind?" She leaned into me, shoulders losing some tension. "Okay. This would help the kids, so I'm willing to consider it seriously."

I kissed her forehead gratefully. We were in this together. With patience and compromise on both sides, Lucia's addition could represent a new foundation of mutual understanding, rather than lost independence. All transitions came with growing pains, but love would light the way.

Later, I went to talk to Mom while she tidied up. As Lucia put the throw pillows in their places, her voice broke through my thoughts, startlingly clear and strong. "You know, I've been thinking a lot about us living together. It might actually be exciting." I turned, surprised by her tone. Her face was bright with an unexpected optimism. "I mean, think about it," Lucia continued, a spark in her eyes. "I could contribute to the household in ways I haven't had the chance to before. Financially, sure, but also just being there for the kids, for Rachel, for you." Rachel, who had come into the room and had been quietly listening, glanced at Lucia, her eyes softening. "You really think it'll work?" Lucia nodded vigorously. "I do. It's about having a little faith, right? I've always felt a little lonely since Daniel moved out to college, and this feels right. We're strong together." I watched Rachel's face, saw the tension ease as Lucia spoke. Lucia's enthusiasm, her willingness to contribute and her faith in us as a family, was contagious. "And hey," Lucia added with a gentle smile towards Rachel, "we'll make it work. Together. With boundaries and respect. I promise."

Rachel's smile, hesitant at first, grew more confident. I felt a warm sense of hope blooming in the room. This wasn't just about making do; it was about building something together, something new and full of potential. I couldn't help but feel proud of Lucia's change in perspective and her genuine offer to help. It wasn't just about the practicalities. Her words carried a weight of commitment and care, a reassurance that she was in this with us, wholeheartedly. "Yeah," I said, finding my voice. "Together. We can make this work."

In that moment, I knew that whatever challenges lay ahead, we were ready to face them. Not just as individuals, but as a united family. Each of us would bring our own strengths and perspectives to the table. Lucia's readiness to embrace this change was more than just a gesture; it was a testament to her character, her kindness, and her belief in us as a family.

I couldn't help but feel proud of Lucia's change in perspective and her genuine offer to help. It wasn't just about the practicalities. Her words carried a weight of commitment and care, a reassurance that she was in this with us, wholeheartedly. "Yeah," I said, finding my voice. "Together. We can make this work."

In that moment, I knew that whatever challenges lay ahead, we were ready to face them. Not just as individuals, but as a united family. Each of us would bring our own strengths and perspectives to the table. Lucia's readiness to embrace this change was more than just a gesture; it was a testament to her character, her kindness, and her belief in us as a family

Building Bonds and Bridges

Rachel

The afternoon light filtering into the kitchen cast a warm glow as I waited for the kettle to boil. I leaned back against the counter, letting the quiet settle my swirling thoughts. Making a pot of chamomile tea had become my daily ritual. It was a small way to reclaim time for myself in the midst of our chaotic family life Soon this kitchen would be demolished, and the walls would be knocked down to make way for the new addition.

Our cramped but cozy home would be transformed, forever. The thought still felt overwhelming, though. After weeks of planning, the thought was gradually growing on me, and I'd begun to feel excited. I pictured what it would look like. The back wall would be removed to extend the kitchen to twice its current size. There would be space for a large granite-topped island where we could gather as a family for meals. The increased counter space and storage would make preparing dinner much smoother. Especially, when Lucia and I both wanted to be in the kitchen.

Off the new kitchen area, there would be a spacious nursery with warm wood floors. There would be a bay window that would flood with afternoon light. I could envision rocking my baby there, as tree branches swayed outside. Connected to the nursery would be Lucia's suite. It would be a comfy bedroom, living area, and small kitchenette.

She would have a birds-eye view of her grandbaby through the shared wall's window. She would be able to pitch in with midnight feelings, but she would still keep privacy in her own domain.

The downstairs, cramped den would be transformed into a lavish master bath for Daniel and me to share. After so many years of a tiny, outdated bathroom, having a peaceful retreat to relax in a jetted tub would be a dream.

The contractor had shown us scale models highlighting how seamlessly the contemporary addition would blend with our Craftsman-style home's existing structure. Though it still felt monumental envisioning these sweeping changes, I really looked forward to the coming days.

Our once modest house would be beautifully transformed, creating space for each family member's needs without sacrificing intimacy. United through flexibility and compromise, perhaps our relationships would be shaped anew as well. Hopefully we will bond ever closer through weathering this mammoth adjustment together.

The tea kettle whistled, pulling me from my reverie. As I poured water over the dried flowers, their earthy aroma wafted up, unwinding the tension in my shoulders. Cradling the two steaming mugs, I made my way to the sunroom where Lucia sat waiting.

She had her reading glasses on, squinting at a newspaper. Her cane rested against the armchair. "Here we are," I said, the brightness a little forced, though I hoped she wouldn't catch it. I placed the tea on the wicker table between us. Lucia glanced up, folding the paper neatly aside. "Thank you, dear. You didn't have to go to the trouble."

"It's no trouble at all." I settled into the cushioned wicker chair with a contented sigh. Our daily tea had become an unexpected pleasure, a quiet respite before the kids returned from school. For a few moments, we sipped in companionable silence.

I breathed in the soothing vapor, letting it calm my constantly frazzled nerves. Lucia gazed out the large window overlooking the backyard, where a squirrel chased a leaf fluttering in the breeze. "How are you feeling today?" I asked. "That turmeric should help with inflammation." I nodded towards the mug clasped in her wrinkled hands.

"Much better, thanks to you." Lucia gave me a grateful smile. "I don't know what I'd do without these tea sessions in the afternoons." I smiled back, warmed by her sincerity.

Before she came to live with us, I could never have envisioned us bonding like this. She had seemed so intimidating. She was Daniel's formidable mother, who didn't approve of me. Now here we sat, two women navigating their own challenges but finding common ground. Lucia took another long sip of tea, sighing contentedly.

"You know, when Daniel first proposed this addition, I had my doubts." She gave me a knowing look over her glasses. "I could tell you weren't thrilled either." I chuckled. "Was it that obvious?" Lucia nodded, eyes glinting with humor. "Oh, yes. I know my opinionated ways aren't always easy to take. But I'm so glad we've come to this point, Rachel. Getting to know you these past weeks has been a joy."

I felt unexpected tears prickle. "For me as well. I was so scared of losing myself in all this chaos. But you've shown me I don't have to sacrifice everything." Lucia leaned forward, patting my hand gently. "Nor should you, dear girl. You're allowed to want your own life."

Her warm understanding loosened something in my chest. I shared quietly, "I was afraid your expectations for how I should raise the kids would overwhelm me. Daniel always spoke so glowingly about your parenting style." "Nonsense," Lucia tutted. "How you mother those children is your business. I'm just here to lend support, and drink tea."

She tipped her mug at me playfully. I laughed, relief flooding through me. With compassion and open communication, we had moved past misconceptions into mutual trust and respect. We spent the next hour chatting about baby names, decorating ideas for the nursery, and her favorite memories as a young mom.

The conversation flowed smoothly, punctuated by warm laughter. Too soon, I heard the front door bang open, followed by the sounds of the kids throwing off their backpacks and shoes. Lucia and I exchanged a smile tinged with regret. Our peaceful interlude was ending.

But as I gathered the mugs to rinse out in the kitchen, I realized the warm glow inside me lingered. Spending this time getting to know Lucia felt like finding the missing piece. I had expected her presence to be a burden, her advice intrusive. But she had given me something much more valuable. She had become a confidante, a mentor, and maybe even a friend.

Our families joining together would require work and sacrifice, but it could also open up new wells of support. With open hearts, this unusual living situation might foster more joy than any of us could have predicted. Later we were all gathered in the unfinished nursery.

We took in the smell of fresh paint and sawdust that lingered in the air. Plastic tarps covered the floor, and drywall panels leaned against the studded walls. But déjà vu swept over me as I watched the kids take it all in with wide eyes.

Just like when we first moved in with Daniel and his children, hope and potential lived here amidst the disarray. "Here's where we'll put the crib, near the window," I said, pointing. "The rocking chair will go right by it for late night feedings."

"Ooh, can I help decorate?" Amy asked, bouncing on her toes. "I can paint yellow flowers. I smiled, smoothing down her unruly curls. "Of course, sweetie. Yellow, if it's a girl." "Oh, then blue, if it's a boy."

"I like blue. I'll help, too." Michael chimed in, just as excited. I smile at the two younger kids. "We'll all decorate together." Sandra trailed her fingers over the smooth framing studs. "Hard to believe there was no room here before. Kind of amazing." "It is amazing!" My normally reserved stepdaughter's eyes were bright. She believed in this change, in what we could build together.

Michael suddenly pushed past us, legs pumping as he raced from one end of the room to the other. "This place is HUGE! Way bigger than my room!" His voice echoed off the bare rafters. I laughed. "Well, it has to fit all the new baby stuff, silly." Daniel slid an arm around my waist. "I think he approves. I know I do." He pressed a kiss to my temple.

Lucia eased herself down on a folded tarp with her cane. She gazed around, satisfied. "You all have done remarkably well. I look forward to meeting my newest grandchild here." Pride swelled in my chest. Honestly, it still felt like a dream some days. But we had pushed through doubts and obstacles to turn Daniel's vision into reality.

"Alright troops, time to clear out so the nice contractors can work," Daniel said, clapping his hands. The kids groaned but obediently filed out, chattering excitedly about the nursery.

Soon, only Lucia and I remained amidst the sawdust and drop cloths. She eased herself up slowly, wincing.

"The tea helps, but these old joints still ache." She waved off my offered arm. "Now, what's this I hear about you going back to work?"

I nodded. "Just part-time at first. With you here to help out, it feels manageable." I laid a hand on my rounded belly. "And it'll be good for me to do something for myself again."

Lucia squeezed my shoulder with surprising strength. "Good for you. You're an excellent mother, but also your own person." She tilted her head. "You know, I could watch the little ones if you ever wanted to get coffee with new mom friends. No need to only socialize with this old bat."

I laughed. "I appreciate that. But I love our talks." Impulsively, I pulled her into a hug. She stiffened, then relaxed, patting my back gently.

"Let go of your fears," I said softly. "We're in this together."

Lucia's eyes glistened behind her glasses. "Yes, together."

Arm in arm, we made our way downstairs. The kids were sprawled on the living room floor, playing with blocks and dolls. Well, most of them were.

Michael sat apart, frowning as he smashed two trucks together aggressively.

"Hey, Mikey, are you okay?"

He barely glanced up at me and grunted a response. I paused for a moment, wondering if he was okay.

I went back to my task but made a mental note to spend one on-one time with him soon.

He was probably feeling displaced. After all, he was the baby before all this started.

For now, I soaked up the bustling sounds of my family enjoying a lazy Saturday with grilled fish and fries.

The coming months would bring sleepless nights, and new challenges. But together, we would provide this new addition to our lives with enough love and care to withstand anything.

A few days later, I bustled around the kitchen, getting snacks ready for the kids before starting dinner.

They'd just returned from school and their chatter had woken me from an afternoon doze. Feeling a little tired, I'd decided we could have some snacks, so I could push dinner a little later. Maybe I'd just call Daniel to pick up pizza when he closed.

"Michael, Amy, Sandra, come have some snacks!" I called. The girls came thundering down the stairs, but Michael didn't appear.

"Where's your brother?" I asked Sandra. She shook her head. "Haven't seen him."

Placing the dishcloth I held aside, I searched all the usual spots. I searched the playroom, backyard, and his bedroom. My heart beat faster as I went out to the pool area and backyard.

There was no sign of him. Fear gripped my chest.

Grabbing the phone, I called Daniel, my words tumbling out in a rush. "Michael's gone, I can't find him anywhere, I've looked all over."

"Okay, stay calm," Daniel said firmly. "I'll leave work and look around the neighborhood." I hung up, close to tears. Sandra tentatively said, "You know, he loves hanging out in the toy section at the mall."

Of course! Why hadn't I thought of that? "Lucia, can you come with me? I'll let Daniel know so he can meet us there too." She hurried to grab her purse and cane. "Let's go find our boy."

Her calm determination steadied me as we rushed out. "Sandra, you and Amy be careful, and if Michael shows up, call either of us immediately." She nodded numbly and pulled Amy close.

I drove just below the city limit even though the distance was only a seven-minute walk. Once at the mall, Lucia and I split up to cover more ground. The garishly bright toy store blurred through my panicked tears. Then I spotted a small figure hunched by the trucks, shaggy blond head bent.

"Michael!" I cried. He looked up, lower lip wobbling. I ran over and swept him into my arms. "You scared us, honey; don't run off like that!"

"You don't want me anymore," he choked out. "You only love the new baby now." My heart shattered. "Oh sweetie, no, of course that's not true! We love you so much."

I texted Daniel that I had found Michael just as Lucia came hurrying over. Her lined face softened with relief at the sight of us.

Security escorted us to the service elevators so we could exit discreetly. As the doors slid closed and the elevator jerked downward, Lucia said gently, "Let's all have ice cream after dinner and have some family time. Would you like that, Michael?"

He nodded, scrubbing at his tear-stained cheeks with a small fist. Just then, the elevator ground to a halt between floors. The lights flickered off, casting us in dim emergency lighting.

"What's happening?" Michael asked in a small voice. I forced my own panic down, keeping my tone calm. I reached a hand to hold his in mine.

"It's okay, sometimes elevators get stuck, but it's not dangerous." I pushed the call button to notify security. Lucia's calm demeanor also helped lessen Michael's worry as we waited in the cramped space.

Trying to distract him, she asked, "Shall I tell a story? When your daddy was young, we would make up tales on long car rides." Michael perked up at hearing about his dad's childhood. As Lucia wove an amusing tale, the atmosphere brightened. When she finished, peaceful silence descended.

Then Lucia said quietly, "You know, I haven't always been the best at showing it, but I care deeply for this family."

She looked at me earnestly. "For you, Rachel. I know I was critical before, but that came from wanting to protect Daniel. I see now that you bring out the best in him and in all of us."

Her words released a tension I hadn't realized I still carried. "Having you here will be such a gift," I said. "For me, and the kids."

Lucia patted my hand. "We mothers have to stick together. I'm here for you, whatever comes."

Michael chimed in from his perch on my lap, "We'll be best friends!"

We all chuckled. As the elevator shuddered back to life, gliding downward, a sense of peace enveloped me. We would move into the future, joint but stronger, bonded by care and understanding.

Daniel was waiting anxiously outside the mall entrance when the elevator doors finally opened.

"Daddy!" Michael cried, sprinting into his open arms.

"Oh buddy, you're okay," Daniel breathed, hugging him tight. He looked up at me, eyes bright with emotion, mouthing "Thank you."

I just shook my head, overwhelmed with relief. Lucia and I hung back slightly, allowing them a moment.

Daniel finally released Michael. "Let's all head home," he said, hoisting a grateful Michael in his arms.

Once home, the girls crowded around for hugs, lecturing Michael not to scare them like that again. Their concern came out as bossiness, but underneath you could see how much they loved their little brother.

After dinner, we all shared large bowls of ice cream, as a family. The girls headed upstairs to finish their homework; casting concerned looks back at their brother. Meanwhile, Daniel sat on the couch with Michael curled into his side.

"Hey buddy, can we talk about what happened?" Daniel asked gently. Michael's lower lip quivered. "We just want to understand so we can help you," I added, sitting on Michael's other side and stroking his hair.

In a small voice, he said, "The new baby is more 'portant now." Fat tears spilled down his cheeks. "You don't need me."

Daniel and I exchanged anguished looks over his bent head. How could our bright, vivacious boy think he didn't matter?

"Oh sweetheart, the new baby won't change how very much we love you," I assured him. "This family only works because of everyone in it, especially you."

Daniel hugged Michael close. "You're my big guy. I'll always need you." Michael offered a tremulous smile.

Lucia, who had been watching nearby, came over and opened her arms. Michael climbed onto her lap. "I'm so sorry we made you feel left out," Lucia said. "From now on, you and I will have special days together, just us. Would you like that?"

"Can we bake cookies?" Michael asked, perking up. "All the cookies your heart desires," Lucia promised. "And the baby can have the burned ones!" Michael said with a giggle.

Laughter echoed around the room, lifting the gloom. Later, after Michael was sleeping, Daniel wrapped his arms around me from behind. "Long day, but we survived."

I leaned back into his solid strength with a tired sigh. "We certainly did." Daniel nuzzled into my hair. "I'm so proud of you.

Most women would fall apart with everything on your plate. But here you are, holding us together." His faith in me never failed to spark warmth in my chest.

I turned and cupped his stubbled cheek. "Only because I have you by my side. We're a team, remember?" "Always." Daniel drew me close and kissed me deeply. For a blissful moment, nothing else mattered except the two of us.

The next morning, I came out of the bedroom to the smell of sizzling bacon and Lucia's low humming. She squeezed my shoulder affectionately. "You sit. Let me make breakfast for the family this morning."

As she bustled around the kitchen, it hit me that a few months ago, I couldn't have envisioned us this way. Lucia had become as much a part of our lives as any relative. And her presence would continue keeping us afloat through the coming rollercoaster of new parenthood. With open hearts, we had found strength in each other.

Our family was woven together by bonds that were both old and new. But the powerful cords joining us felt strong enough now to weather any coming storm. The baby continued to grow as we anticipated his arrival.

The August sun beat down on us as Lucia and I sat swinging gently on the back patio. Daniel had gone to the store for a few items. We sipped icy lemonade, watching the kids splash wildly in the pool. Their joyful shouts mingled with the cicadas' humming chorus.

"Can you believe summer's nearly over?" Lucia mused. "Feels like we just blinked and suddenly school is starting up again." I smiled ruefully, running a hand over my rounded belly. "It's flown by. Before we know it, this little one will be keeping us up all night."

Lucia patted my knee with a knowing look. "You're in for an adventure. But the love makes it worthwhile."

We relaxed in a comfortable silence as a light breeze stirred the windchimes. Lucia seemed to be pondering something. Finally, she spoke, a touch hesitantly. "Rachel, I know I didn't fully welcome you into this family, in the beginning. But I want you to know that has changed. You've become very dear to me." I squeezed her hand, and then I touched it. "And you to me, Lucia."

She nodded, blinking away a sheen in her eyes. "I know. I see it in how you include me and ask my advice about the baby as if I were your own mother."

Lucia took a steadying breath. "Which is why I want you to have this." She drew a black velvet box from her dress pocket and placed it in my palm. Nestled inside was a stunning antique necklace, it was an oval peridot stone surrounded by smaller diamonds, on a delicate golden chain.

I gasped, tears prickling unexpectedly. "This is too precious; I can't accept it," I stammered. Lucia closed my fingers around it. "It belonged to my grandmother, and then to my mother, and now I want you to have it. A family heirloom for my newest daughter." Her voice caught on the last word. "Oh Lucia."

At a loss for words, I embraced her fiercely. She clung to me just as tightly. Finally drawing back, Lucia dabbed at her eyes and said briskly, "Here now, let's see how it looks." With trembling fingers, I clasped the necklace around my neck. The peridot pendant rested just above my heart, glinting in the sunlight.

Lucia took my hands in hers. "Perfect. You wear it beautifully, my dear." I had to blink back fresh tears. "I don't know what to say. Thank you; this means the world to me." "You don't have to say anything." Lucia smiled, her eyes crinkling. "Just know you have become like family to me. Truly."

On impulse, I hugged her again, overcome with emotion.

I couldn't have dreamed the formidable Lucia would ever accept me so completely. "I always wanted a mother's guidance," I admitted thickly. "You've filled that role for me and for our children."

Lucia stroked my hair, voice unsteady. "And you've given Daniel and me warmth and joy again. Our lives are so much richer with you in them." As we held each other, the gulf of old tensions and misunderstandings seemed to close fully, at last. United in our shared love for this family, Lucia and I could now face the future as true partners.

Later, Daniel noticed the necklace as I cleared the dinner plates. He came up behind me at the sink, fingers brushing lightly over the pendant. "This is my mother's. She's always loved it. It's so exquisite." I leaned back into him. "Your mother gave it to me earlier today. Can you believe it? She gave me a family heirloom."

Daniel kissed my neck. "She must really love you. I'm so thankful to have two strong, incredible women as the heart of our family." I twined my fingers with his, our matching rings glinting. With so much uncertainty ahead, this connection was my anchor. It bound me to Daniel, Lucia, and the family we were nurturing together. "We're so lucky," I whispered. And though the coming months would test us again, I knew we could weather any storm. Side by side, and hand in hand

Anticipation and Preparation

Daniel

My phone buzzed with another client text, just as I walked bleary-eyed into the kitchen. I barely glanced up from composing a quick reply, as I grabbed my usual black coffee and protein bar.

"Whoa, watch it!" Rachel yelped. I narrowly avoided colliding with her, not having noticed her bent figure rummaging through a lower cabinet.

One hand braced her lower back while the other attempted to lift a cast iron skillet.

"Oh geez, I'm so sorry hon," I said, sliding my phone away. "Let me get that."

I easily extracted the heavy pan, placing it on the counter before dropping a kiss on her hair. "How'd you sleep?"

"Hardly at all," Rachel grunted, one hand cradling her swollen belly. "Your son thinks my ribs make great kickboxing practice at 3 AM apparently."

Guilt pricked me. My workload has spiked crazily the past month. I'd taken to working in the home office well into the night and leaving before sunrise.

Rachel was nearing the end of this pregnancy and was raising three kids alone.

My phone vibrated with yet another client text. I quickly typed up an acknowledgment before sliding the phone away, refocusing on rubbing Rachel's lower back.

"Sorry, work has just nonstop lately. I know I've been distracted." I sighed, feeling a pang of guilt. "But hey, your checkup is today, right? What time should I meet you there?"

Rachel offered a small smile that didn't reach her eyes. "Yeah, at 2 PM. But don't worry about it if you're too busy."

"I'll be there," I interjected. "Nothing is more important than hearing our son's heartbeat."

I squeezed her shoulder, wishing I could erase the thinly veiled hurt in her eyes after so many weeks of my divided attention. This appointment was a chance to show her she remained priority one.

At 1:45 PM, I slipped quietly out of a budget meeting, phone already dialing Rachel. Her voicemail picked up. I left a quick apology about being stuck in an urgent conference call.

"I'm so sorry, hon, I'm still trapped in this meeting. But could you ask Mom to maybe go with you, instead? Text me how it goes. Love you."

I pictured Rachel's crestfallen face listening to that message. She needed me today.

Protectively cradling her own growing bump in the sterile exam room with only Lucia beside her was no substitute. Self disgust and helplessness warred within me.

Later, as I scrolled through the photos from the appointment, I saw our son stretching languidly, tiny features already so loved. The bittersweet moment I'd sacrificed pierced my heart. "He's so beautiful, honey. Thank you for adding this gift to our family."

Guilt flooded my heart again. Duty shouldn't rob me of being fully present for those that mattered most. I had to fix this imbalance before it was too late. I would, once I reduced this work load on my desk.

That night after the kids were finally asleep, Rachel found me hunched over my laptop at the kitchen table surrounded by case files.

Weariness tugged at my soul, but the work was endless.

Without a word, she firmly rotated the screen down, then eased onto my lap, cradling my stubbled face to her chest. I breathed her in, my tension draining away.

"We need to talk priorities, honey," Rachel finally said into the quiet darkness.

I sighed, the unspoken tension of recent months a weight between us. "You're right. I'm barely keeping my head above water. Maybe once the baby comes."

"That's too long to keep struggling like this." Rachel's fingers stroked my hair. "What if you ask about working remotely for a while until I deliver?"

I leaned back to meet her earnest gaze. "That would help ease being away from you all so much. It's worth proposing, at least."

Rachel smiled softly, touching her forehead to mine. In that peaceful embrace, I remembered what I was working so hard for. This was for my family, surrounding me with their steadfast love.

"I promise that you and our kids will come first," I whispered against her lips before kissing her, deeply.

Tomorrow and its unknowns could wait. Tonight was for recalibrating priorities with Rachel curled sweetly in my arms.

We continued to get ready for the baby's arrival. I gripped the edge, steadying it so Lucia could reach to screw in the crib's final side rail. Her silver blond bun bobbed with concentration.

Rachel sat nearby, one hand absently stroking her swollen belly as she supervised my mom's crib assembly knowledgeably. "Little more to the left, mom," she guided. "Yep, now it's lined up perfectly with the mattress base."

"Are you sure we shouldn't hire a contractor for this intricate work?" Lucia huffed, wrinkles creasing as she squinted up at me.

I chuckled, while slotting in the rail and tightening the bolt. "We got this, Mom. It'll mean more with the baby's family building her first bed."

Satisfied with our handiwork, we stepped back to admire the completed crib in the freshly painted nursery. Pale purple walls with stenciled woodland creatures surrounded the cherrywood haven awaiting its occupant's arrival soon.

Rachel squeezed my hand, eyes glistening. Lucia set a gentle palm on the slope of Rachel's belly. "Won't be long now till we're holding him,"

Lucia murmured gently. During that last exam, we discovered the baby would be a boy.

We decided to name him "Luke", in honor of Lucia. The naked emotion in her voice made my own eyes prickle. Three generations bound by this new fragile life. Past and future were colliding in a poignant full circle.

Later in the half-finished kitchen, sawdust mingling with mouthwatering aromas of roasting turkey, we gathered around makeshift tables lying atop contractor buckets. "To family, both joined by blood and choice." I lifted my Solo cup of sparkling cider, my smile encompassing Rachel, Lucia, and the kids. "Being together, that's what matters most."

Rachel's brown eyes glowed in the construction string lights draped overhead. "Dig in, everyone, before the food gets cold!" Lucia admonished. Chuckles echoed as serving spoons scraped heaping portions of her famous Thanksgiving spread onto our mismatched plates.

Scarcely a month later, we joined each other in the plastic shrouded nursery room, again. I held up two color swatches, debating. "So should the name sign be watermelon or actual newborn's pink?" "Darling, you must consider aesthetics.

The melon will clash horribly with the lavender," Lucia scolded mildly, continuing to fold neat stacks of Luke's new cotton onesies and footie pajamas in the dresser. I shot a teasing grin sideways at Rachel. "Dang, decorating a baby's room is no joke with these two!" She laughed, shaking her head indulgently at Lucia's baby outfit color coordination and my paint matching efforts.

Two weeks after the final coat of paint dried in the bedroom adjoining the nursery, we reveled in the fresh woodsy scent. The windows were thrown open to the crisp night. Moonlight lined the cozy nest awaiting late night cries and early feeds, blending the eerie beauty of expectant silence with anticipation.

There was an undercurrent permeating each mundane task completed, bringing us even closer together. Laying curled together, tracing my fingers over Rachel's taut belly, feeling tiny flutters within, I whispered a fervent prayer. *"God, please bless us. Please let this birth be a healthy one and give us the grace to face everything together. Amen."*

I pulled up to the house after a long Saturday at the office, gathering client files from the passenger seat. Through the living room window, I noticed the lights seemed brighter than usual.

This was odd for mid-evening, with the whole family already home. Balancing my briefcase, I nudged open the front door. "Honey, sorry I'm late but..."

"Surprise!" a boisterous chorus erupted as I stepped inside. I jolted, files spilling onto the hardwood floors. A room full of grinning female faces surrounded a stunned Rachel perched on the sofa.

"What?" I blinked dumbly, taking in the pink and blue streamers festooning our living room. A handmade banner declared "Oh, Baby!" in bubbly script.

The pastor's wife, Wendy, swept forward, enveloping me in a scented embrace. "There's daddy himself! So sorry to startle you, but we wanted to celebrate Baby Luke's impending arrival with your lovely family." "And by family, we mean Rachel of course," Lucia interjected wryly, appearing at my elbow with a glass of sparkling cider.

"You menfolk stay upstairs and keep grooming those beards or whatever it is you do." Amidst the bubbly laughter, I felt a responding grin stretch my stubbled cheeks. Pastel-swaddled neighborhood ladies occupied every seat, many were familiar churchgoers.

There were even a few colleagues of mine. I spotted my secretary, Janice, scanning a table bearing tiny sandwiches and frosted cookies. Oh, that's why she'd asked to leave the office early. "How in the world did you ladies orchestrate all this?" I asked.

"I may have made a few strategic calls," Lucia admitted. "Rachel deserves to be cherished during this sacred season." Her eyes softened.

I looked at my wife as she gently fielded effusive baby advice from grey-haired matrons.

"Well, this is incredibly thoughtful, mom," I said, blinking sudden moisture from my eyes. I pressed a swift kiss to her powdered cheek. "I'll leave you to it." Gathering my spilled paperwork, I retreated upstairs marveling at the sisterhood community.

From my office, I heard peals of laughter intermittently floating up the stairwell. This was amidst Lucia's lilting accent as she held court. Around dinnertime, a soft knock preceded Wendy peeking inside my man-cave sanctuary. "We're serving cake if you'd like to sneak down for a slice. I know it's ladies-only, technically..."

I waved off her apology. "I don't need to crash the party. But maybe send some up with Rachel if she needs a break?" Wendy nodded, eyes crinkling knowingly. "Oh, I suspect she's quite enjoying being the belle of the ball.

But Lucia keeps plying her with Mocktails and tiny quiches so I'm sure your bride appreciates the respite offer." Sure enough, half an hour later I heard labored footsteps on the stairs before Rachel appeared clutching a groaning paper plate capped by a pink iced confection complete with a plastic stork.

Kicking the door shut behind her with one foot, she sank onto my leather office couch with an exaggerated huff.

I rescued the tipping cake slice just in time. "Rough job you got there, being so popular?" I teased.

"Oh, hush. Yes, okay. It's been surprisingly fun." Rachel's glowing smile gave away her delight at the community pampering. "Your mom somehow managed to invite every woman I've ever met, though!"

I settled beside her, drawing Rachel's tired feet into my lap and kneading firmly. She groaned in bliss around a huge bite of frosting.

"Well, you deserve to be cherished like the queen you are, for everything you manage so gracefully, always." I lifted her hand to brush a soft kiss over her knuckles, our engraved bands glinting.

Downstairs faint shrieks erupted amidst humming chatter. Rachel quirked one brow, amusement glinting through her fatigue. "Sounds like Lucia initiated Baby Bingo. I should probably get back to the madness!"

Capturing one last private moment, I pulled my wife close, thrilled at her unrestrained joy. As Rachel descended to rejoin the revelry awaiting, I sent up quiet thanks for this family. Knowingly or not, this union lifted burdens through camaraderie and laughter, right when we needed it most.

The baby shower lasted another hour. After the last guest had gone, Rachel sank onto the sofa and slept.

A couple of days later, after I returned from work, Rachel came out of the bedroom and sat slowly onto the leather couch with a muffled groan. She had one hand braced on her lower back.

I cast a sharp glance as I set my briefcase down. "Honey, are you okay? I thought the pain meds were helping? It hasn't even been four hours since you told me you'd taken them."

"Yeah, they took the edge off for a bit, but the pain is back." Rachel tried a wan smile that quickly twisted into a grimace. "Probably just standard late pregnancy stuff. Only six weeks to go." I moved behind her, kneading gently up her rigid spine.

Rachel began to complain of relentless back and abdomen aches the past few days, ever since the surprise shower. When she winced again, I stated firmly, "I think I'd better get you to the hospital, honey."

I grabbed my keys, calling out to the family that we were stepping out and would be back in a while. I didn't want the family to worry, but when Lucia came out, I whispered to her where we would be going.

Ten minutes later, Rachel was lying on the examination bed, and the doctor had just come in for the check-up. "Just breathe, nice and slow," Dr. Emir instructed, moving the ultrasound wand steadily over the taut skin of Rachel's belly.

I gripped her hand, eyes glued to the screen's grayscale image. The rapid lub-dub of our son's steady heart beat echoed in the exam room.

Rachel flinched, face contorting. "Sorry, having some cramping again," she explained tightly to the doctor.

Dr Emir clicked a button, freezing the image. He spun on his stool to face us, features creasing with concern beneath his greying mustache. "The cramping is worrisome, combined with what you've shared about ongoing back pain recently."

He steepled his fingers. "It could signal preterm labor." My breath caught sharply. I blurted, "But he's only thirty-four weeks along. Is the baby in danger if he delivers early?" Rachel's eyes rounded with fear as her fingers constricted mine.

"At this stage, the chances of healthy lung development are quite favorable," the doctor hastened to reassure us. "We'll simply monitor closely for progression into active labor. Contractions, bleeding, water breaking; those are red flags to get back here promptly."

I exhaled shakily. "So basically, just take it easy and wait and see?" Dr Emir offered an encouraging smile beneath his thick mustache. "Essentially. What you're experiencing is prodromal labor. The body is gearing up. Stay hydrated; rest on your left side; and try not to worry."

Rachel nodded bravely, but I glimpsed the shadow of anxiety lurking in her eyes that surely mirrored my own. We still had critical preparations to complete before welcoming this child to earth-side.

She seemed to experience some relief, but a couple of days later, I lay beside my wife late at night and observed her strained expression. "Have you timed how often the bouts hit, at least?" I asked.

Rachel shook her head, face mashed into a throw pillow. "No real pattern that I can tell. Feels almost constant today, though."

I continued the deep tissue massage helplessly, anxiety gnawing my gut. Lord, please let her discomfort stop, and give her peace. We weren't ready yet for Luke's dramatic entrance. A few hours later I inventoried supplies in the slowly coming together nursery. Paint fumes mingled with new crib aroma. My hammering pulse gradually settled. We could make this work even if the baby insisted on an early debut.

Heading downstairs seeking dinner, I found Rachel hunched at the kitchen table gripping a mug of cooling tea. My morning's optimism vanished seeing the strain carving new lines beside her pinched mouth. "Hey, why didn't you call me?" I murmured, at once resuming counterpressure against her fist-sized lower back knots. Rachel exhaled harshly. "You were busy. I didn't want to..."

She trailed off, flinching as another spasm seized her abdomen. I swept sweaty hair off her clammy forehead with rising urgency. "That's it, we're getting you checked out again."

"Daniel, I'm sure it's nothing," Rachel protested even as she struggled upright. "Humor me," I countered gently.

Something felt off. This was beyond standard late term woes. Time to rule out early labor.

At the Emergency Room, the maternal health doctor performed another irritatingly thorough exam before confirming things seemed intact after all. I asked about monitoring Rachel longer, given the unrelenting pain. But he shrugged off her symptoms as typical for pre-labor. He recommended that we simply return if contractions turned regular.

The ride home passed in tense silence. I could sense Rachel's embarrassment at dragging us out twice now for what amounted to Braxton Hicks false alarms in the end. My halfhearted attempts at optimism remained unconvincing even to myself. Until Luke's safe arrival I knew we'd both be plagued by niggling doubt and dread. And the need for a lot of prayer. Back home Lucia took immediate charge, banishing an ashen Rachel to bed rest while directing me to massage her lower extremities and apply hot compresses for the muscle spasms.

Only after ensuring her daughter-in-law was as comfortable as possible did Lucia allow me to help hastily throw together a pasta dinner for the kids. We moved in harmonious culinary synchronicity. She chopped vegetables; I grated the cheese and whisked the sauce. This was truly an improvised, nurturing ballet, honed organically during this past year living together.

With Rachel finally sleeping soundly post pain pill, and thanks to Lucia's soothing ministrations, I sank into the rocking chair I'd assembled earlier that day, tipping my face gratefully toward divine aid. However overwhelming, these temporary trials nurtured patience and trust that we'd soon embrace in the sweetest deliverance swaddled in innocence.

Faithful Creator would finish the work He had begun in us despite our faltering footsteps. I continued to pray, and at some point, must have fallen asleep because I jerked awake to unfamiliar noises in the dark.

I heard a rhythmic creaking, mingling with muted groans. Adrenaline flooding my system, I fumbled the bedside lamp on. Rachel was nowhere beside me. Another low moan sounded from the direction of the rocking chair near the nursery doorway.

I vaulted from bed and rushed over to find Rachel bent forward gripping the curved wooden arms, knuckles blanched. "Rachel...?" I whispered hoarsely. "What's going on, why are you out of bed?" Eyes squeezed shut, she panted through gritted teeth, "My water broke while I was peeing. Then, the contractions started right away."

She groaned again, the cords in her neck taut. I gripped her shoulder, pulse racing out of control. "Broke? But, but, why didn't you wake me immediately?" Rachel shook her head jerkily, hair stuck to her sweat dampened cheeks. She puffed. "You needed rest. I thought they might stop, but they keep coming faster."

Dread congealed in my gut like day old oatmeal. I dashed for the phone, nearly fumbling with typing 911. But before I could hit send, Rachel cried out. "Daniel wait; something feels wrong. I need to push."

I froze; the receiver was clutched in my suddenly nerveless fingers. This couldn't be happening yet. "What? No don't push yet, just keep breathing," I babbled, rushing back over.

Wild scenarios of dangerous preterm deliveries crowded my panic-stricken thoughts. But Rachel was past logic, every sinew coiled towards a primal goal. "Get towels. I can feel him coming," she gasped.

Realizing emergency responders would arrive too late, my paramedic training kicked in. This happened despite the panicking husband and father in me railing helplessly. I raced for clean sheets then knelt before my straining wife. It now registered that she was dressed only in a thin nightshirt, and this nightshirt was rucked up over her hugely distended abdomen. "You're doing amazing, just breathe," I coached through numb lips, reaching to check her progress.

Rachel's face contorted with each relentless contraction as screams tore from her throat. I clung to her hand impotently, the prenatal training failing woefully in the face of seeing the woman I loved in such prolonged agony.

Outside, lightning cracked through the roiling night sky, and thunder echoed the tumultuous storm that raged within these walls.

Then suddenly, the light blinked several times, then darkness engulfed the room. The power had cut out, cutting all illumination except ghostly shadows cast sporadically by the fire I'd hastily lit earlier. My heart stuttered in my chest. No power meant no way to adequately see or sterilize equipment or heat water. Fear congealed like icy sludge in my veins.

What if Luke didn't make it to the earthside safely because of my faltering? Rachel needed me to be strong now when she had nothing left to give. Swallowing panic, I grabbed the flashlight from the emergency kit, at the same time yelling to Lucia to get flashlights for the children.

I cast the beam over her blood-streaked thighs and the white sheets that were bunched under Rachel's bent knees. Her face glistened greyish in the ambient light glow, etched with torment, but it was set with grim determination riding each cresting peak.

"He's coming too fast!" Rachel sobbed, sweat pouring off her contorted face. My large hands guided our son's slippery entrance gently, despite the violent trembling. "You got this. Keep pushing!" I choked past the overwhelming emotions flooding every sense. At last, the tiny purple-tinged crown emerged, and then retreated between pushes, turning my marrow to jelly once more.

But under Lucia's low murmured encouragement and my awed coaching, Rachel rallied herself unbelievably further. With a primal roar, she bore down, utterly spent. I caught Luke's slippery body just as the lights suddenly flickered back on.

His thin reedy cries were the sweetest sound ever to pierce that charged air. Hardly daring to breathe, I wrapped Rachel and the wailing baby in soft blankets. Joy and relief left me utterly wrecked. Through hellfire we traveled to this glorious birth, but nothing could shake the foundations of family forged in unconditional love.

Hardly breathing, I rested the writhing infant on Rachel's bare chest. "Ohhh, Luke," she exhaled in wonder. Her arms curled protectively despite the residual tremors from her lightning quick labor.

I could only stare agape at this miraculous being, especially considering I'd been asleep fifteen minutes ago. Gingerly, I wrapped mother and son in soft sheets just as Lucia came rushing back in.

"How's the baby?" She leaned to take a look at the baby, then began to gather the bloodied towels. Rachel's pale face was spent, but she proudly cradled a mewling bundle to her breast.

"Little Luke couldn't wait for the hospital," I croaked past the wreckage in my throat. I gently pushed sweaty curls off Rachel's ashen face. "You were amazing; he's perfect."

Despite arriving early, Luke seemed to be breathing fine on his own, as we waited anxiously for medical evaluation. Lucia clasped Rachel's hand tightly, silent tears tracking through the wrinkles time had wrought. But for once, her weathered face glowed with unrestrained joy as we welcomed new life, rather than just marking another year's passing.

Suddenly, EMTs rushed in to stabilize mom and baby for transport, interrupting our miraculous scene. As we followed the ambulance to the hospital, I gazed down at the sleeping newborn in my arms.

I glanced back at Rachel. She was dozing, exhausted yet peaceful. This child had entered the world in a rush on his own terms, forging bonds between generations in the process. Just maybe, little Luke was the cement to seal our family's foundation firmly into the uncharted future.

A New Beginning

R achel
Hot tears of joy and relief flooded down my face as Daniel laid the wriggling, sticky infant on my heaving chest.

"Rachel, he's absolutely perfect," Daniel whispered reverently, his gaze shimmering with equal emotion. In that spectacular split second, all other cares evaporated. Nothing else mattered, whether it was the unfinished nursery, or my postpartum nursing classes that remained incomplete, or my fears over handling four children.

This tiny fighter nestling into me, as Lucia wrapped us in soft blankets, was the only reality that mattered. Our family of six was finally complete.

Later at the hospital, all tests showed Luke was miraculously healthy despite his dramatic entrance. My overflowing heart nearly burst as I watched Daniel tenderly cradle our swaddled son.

The girls and Michael would be bursting with impatient excitement at home. They were so anxious to meet their new baby brother. Sure enough, as we pulled up the next evening, the front door was flung wide open, spilling cheering children into the snowy yard.

Lucia followed more slowly. She beamed at everyone. Daniel helped me and little Luke inside, to eagerly waiting arms. "He's so cute!" Amy squealed, touching the downy head peeking from his blanket cocoon. "Baby Luke, we will protect you from monsters, okay?"

Watching my three eldest gently pass their brother around the circle, I felt true joy. All lingering anxiety finally released its grip. We were together; we were whole.

We were battle-tested through adversity that only made us stronger. Whatever uncertainties still awaited down unfamiliar roads, I trusted implicitly that our family could weather any storms ahead. We would be linked arm in arm.

I snapped awake. "Shhh...it's alright darling. " I heard Lucia's low murmur through the baby monitor as Luke's angry cries quieted to soft mewls.

Glancing at the glowing red 4:17 AM on my nightstand, I started to throw the covers back, wrestling my sleep-deprived mind awake to handle the latest round of newborn demands. Just then Daniel's slender arm snaked out to restrain me; his face was still mashed into the pillow. "Let your mom take this one. You were up with him at midnight and 2 AM," he mumbled, groggily.

Despite desperately needing more rest, frustration nipped at me hearing Lucia beat me to comforting my son. This made it two nights in a row. But, Daniel was right. I'd been run ragged between the rest of the family and Luke.

With a sigh, I settled back against him, tuning into the baby monitor's transmission again. "...and then the brave knight married the beautiful princess in a magical ceremony..." Lucia shared in a theatrical whisper. I had to smile hearing her regale little Luke with a fairytale at this ungodly hour, instead of just efficiently changing his diaper so everyone could return to bed. She was truly a natural mother.

The next evening, I trudged downstairs after a lingering shower. I discovered music and mingled laughter floating down the hallway from the kitchen. I slowed, relishing the momentarily forgotten sound of my family relaxed and enjoying each other.

I froze at the threshold. Five grinning faces ringed the counter. They were making personalized pizzas. Their hands were dusted white with flour. Even baby Luke was propped happily in his rocker garbling gleefully. Michael noticed me, first. "Hi, Mommy! Look; we are chefs! Nana is teaching us." He waved a lumpen mound of dough proudly. "Good, you're just in time to try my special marinara sauce recipe," Lucia said, deftly sliding a steaming pizza from the oven.

My mouth watered as her savory creation's aroma enveloped me. I ruffled Michael's hair, surprised by the lump constricting my throat. It was wonderful just taking in this bustling scene of connection and joy.

Lucia met my eyes with understanding as she ushered the kids to wash their hands for dinner. She then made me a plate without being asked.

As we later cleaned up together, I realized what a Godsend my mother-in-law had truly become. She offered stability where Daniel and I were struggling just keeping Luke alive.

At least, on some days, which was what it felt like. "Thanks, Mom, for keeping things cheerful," I told Lucia sincerely. "You make everything feel normal and special all at once." She patted my cheek tenderly as if I was young. "You're doing wonderfully, Rachel. This phase is hard for everyone. That's my role here. I keep life running smoothly through the craziness."

Later, as I eased onto the couch exhausted, but cradling a finally sleeping Luke, it hit me. We were all navigating uncharted waters. We were building lives entwined by losses and gains. These spanned years, with linked hearts pulling in sync. With compassion as our guide, together we'd find the shore.

That night, a sharp wail pierced the darkness. I stirred groggily, the exhaustion of early motherhood clouding my mind. Before I could force my leaden body to rise, Daniel was already out of bed, pressing a quick kiss to my tangled hair.

"I've got him," he murmured. With immense relief, I sank back against the pillows while Daniel shuffled to Luke's bassinet. We'd moved the baby to spend the night in our room so Lucia could get a full night's sleep. Through slitted eyes, I saw Daniel lift Luke's tiny body gently, cradling our angry-faced son against his chest. He was breathing in that sweet, milky baby scent I knew so well.

"Shhh. Daddy's got you," Daniel soothed, jiggling lightly as he carried Luke to the rocking chair nearby. Its familiar creak was loud in the peaceful night. As I watched my husband comfort our child so tenderly, gratitude for his steady partnership swelled within me. As Daniel rocked Luke, his head began to nod with sheer exhaustion.

My heart ached seeing the toll this early phase was taking on him, too. Then Sandra appeared silently in the doorway, her face tender with empathy. Without a word, she moved to bundle cranky Luke into her own soft embrace, relieving Daniel momentarily.

Soon Lucia was there as well, guiding a depleted Daniel back under the covers beside me. As she tucked the blankets snugly around us, her tender gaze held decades of motherly memories. Fresh tears prickled unexpectedly behind my eyes.

Whatever uncertainties still awaited us in raising four children, together our family and community would selflessly carry these burdens. Though fiery trials surely awaited down unfamiliar roads, love would light our way each step ahead.

Two months later, I cradled sleeping Luke in my arms, his downy head just peeking out from the heirloom christening gown he wore, as we waited in the vestibule. Faint strains of the pipe organ and murmuring voices drifted from the sanctuary. Beside me, Daniel squeezed my hand, his eyes shining with excitement.

"Ready to officially introduce our little guy to the church?" he asked. I nodded, blinking back a rush of emotion. After so many weeks and sleepless nights parenting a newborn, this long-awaited moment had arrived. We processed slowly down the center aisle behind the pastor, who would be officiating the dedication ritual. I caught glimpses of smiling familiar faces turned to greet our family. There was Lucia, already dabbing at her eyes with a lace handkerchief in the front pew. She was followed by my book club friends waving eagerly from the left row.

Reaching the front, we faced our community. They were gathered to pledge their support in raising this child in a community of faith. Pastor Ephraim turned to us, his kind eyes crinkling as he rested a gentle hand tenderly on Luke's head.

"Little one, we welcome you today into the family of God," his resonant voice filled the hushed sanctuary. "May you come to know Him who formed you, whose Son, our Lord Jesus, gave children a special blessing." He paused before continuing the blessing. "Gracious Father, we dedicate this child to you. Grant him your care and protection. Give him strength to serve you faithfully."

I swallowed the lump in my throat, cradling Luke's sleeping form closer, as the pastor invoked divine presence into his unfolding journey. "Build in him courage, creativity and compassion. May the light of Christ shine through him, drawing others to your love. We pledge as a congregation to nurture and guide this precious life through every season ahead."

Daniel's arm tightened around my shoulders as we bowed heads with the community before the altar. Sunlight from the stained-glass windows bathed us in a kaleidoscope of color. Though the road ahead held unknowns, with this faith family's support we would travel it courageously. A few tears slipped down my cheeks as we handed Luke carefully to Lucia first.

Cradling her newest grandson, her wrinkled face glowed. Daniel's arm encircled me tightly as we watched her whisper a heartfelt blessing over him. Next our other children crowded close for their turn, each offering their own promise to love and teach their baby brother.

Watching solemn Michael take his big brother role seriously, I was reminded again of this family's resilience nurturing each other through life's trials. After the final "Amen", cheers and applause erupted, shaking the vaulted ceiling.

Greeting us afterwards at the front pew, long-time church matrons cooed over sleepy little Luke, nestled safely back in my arms. Promises of home cooked meals and babysitting offers warmed me further as Daniel accepted hearty handshakes from the people around us. Today we celebrated new beginnings entwining generations and a faith family. Though Luke's arrival initially turned my world upside down, this child knit together the very fabric of our community in unexpected ways. Gazing into my baby's tranquil face, joy and possibility seemed endless with these allies cheering our family onward. We were truly, Hearts United In Love.

Dedication

We wouldn't be able to do this for a living if it weren't for our readers. We thank you for reading our books.

Excerpt

Rachel

Hand in hand, we slowly walked out of the courthouse into the bright, spring sunlight. The girls chattered excitedly. I looked down at the documents I clutched. They had the judge's official signature. This completed Sandra's and Michael's adoption.

After almost two years of living as a blended family, it was wonderfully surreal to now be legally bound together. Glancing at Daniel walking beside me, his eyes were bright with emotion behind his glasses.

"So, I guess I can formally call you Mom now?" Sandra spoke up quietly. I turned to see uncharacteristic shyness on my usually reserved stepdaughter's face as she glanced sidelong. My heart caught in my throat. "Oh, sweetie, of course! I would love that more than anything."

Unexpected tears flooded my eyes. Sandra ducked her head, cheeks pinking slightly even as her lips curved upward. Then she leaned into me, whispering "Thanks, Mom."

A joyful sob burst from my chest at that precious word. I folded her tightly in my arms. Daniel wrapped his arms around us both, kissing each of our heads. On Sandra's other side, Amy and Michael crashed into the hug, forming one tangled laughing mass of family.

Right there on the sunny courthouse steps, embraced in blissful unity after weathering so much change together, I finally knew bone-deep that this was truly forever. We belonged to one another for life's every season ahead.

No matter what uncertainties the future held, I trusted our resilient family could overcome anything now - together.

HEARTS UNITED IN LOVE

Love bound this family rooted heart to heart through life's changing seasons; love was their harbor in every storm. We were truly, Hearts United In Love.

65

Afterword

Have you been swept away by Rachel and Daniel's enthusiastic journey from widowhood to love to parenthood?

Their resilient hearts have woven a tapestry of unity, overcoming trials with unwavering affection.

Now, prepare to embark on the next chapter of their lives in <u>Hearts United in Hope</u>, where parenthood unfolds at a new level.

This heart-stirring narrative delves into the joys and challenges every parent cherishes and fears. Witness the unyielding strength a family can cultivate through faith and prayer, even when faced with life's inevitable adversities.

But will tragedy cast a shadow, evaluating the very core of their bond?

Get ready to peek into their world, where laughter mingles with tears, and love perseveres against all odds.

Don't miss out!

Visit the website below and you can sign up to receive emails whenever Karen Kazimer Shockley publishes a new book. There's no charge and no obligation.

https://books2read.com/r/B-A-HIFBB-MNIQD

BOOKS 2 READ

Connecting independent readers to independent writers.

Did you love *Hearts United In Love*? Then you should read *Hearts United in Faith*[1] by Karen Kazimer Shockley!

[2]

Brrrrrrrr. The shrill blare of the alarm clock jolted me awake and out of the thick fog of sleep. I was watching Kathy running in a field of daffodils.

She swung her head, causing her hair to flow over her shoulders, and she laughed. The sound of her voice was clear and melodic, just as I would imagine the voice of a hundred angels singing songs of worship.

Kathy stopped and turned to me. She paused, as though surprised to see me. She smiled and her eyes crinkled in delight. Her whole face lit up with love. She waved at me.

Suddenly, Kathy started to fade away.

---

1. https://books2read.com/u/bP8Q9A

2. https://books2read.com/u/bP8Q9A

"Nooooooo," I yelled, stretching out my hand to grab her and keep her with me for just moments longer.

I wanted to keep holding on to the relief I felt when I was with her.

But even as I said the words, I knew they were wishful. I wasn't making audible sounds.

My eyes snapped open, and I was on my bed, in my dark quiet room. For a moment my body remained frozen.

A tear slid down my cheek. Kathy looked so happy that it deepened my sadness. I sighed.

The way she had laughed in the dream reminded me of a time, some years back, when my wife, Kathy, and I were out at the park. Kathy had wanted us to go on the free fall.

I was reluctant but Kathy dragged me by my hand. "Come on, darling. It'll be fun."

Shaking my head, I'd gone on the ride with her. Kathy was screaming, clutching my hand and laughing wildly at the same time.

She was scared stiff but exhilarated by the experience.

Even as our hair stood vertical from the speed of the fall, I still felt my breath stop. I stared at her twinkling bright eyes, silky blonde hair and full red lips.

Laying in the bed, I could still hear Kathy's laughter echoing in my ears.

The harsh sound of the alarm clock continued to grate on my nerves, and I reached out with a trembling hand and slammed down the snooze button.

The silence that followed was deafening. It was a sudden and sharp contrast that jarred my emotions in every direction.

I lay there in the predawn darkness, my eyes on the ceiling. I felt the ever-lingering flood of grief wash over me like a tidal wave, dragging me down as though it was an anchor tied to my ankle and flung into the deep, blue sea.

I was used to this pattern by now. Any day I dreamed of Kathy like this, I woke up depressed and tears welled up in my eyes. They were as fresh as though Kathy had just passed.

Not today, Dan. Today, you must be strong. Remember the children. For their sake, move forward, make progress.

I nodded, refusing to let the tears fall.

I dragged myself out of bed and stumbled to the window, I pulled back the curtains.

By now the sun was just beginning to rise, casting a warm glow over the rooftops. It seemed as reluctant to start its day as I was reluctant to face it. Even at that, the beauty of the sunrise did nothing to ease the pain in my heart.

I closed my eyes and took a deep breath. I turned away from the window and walked over to the dresser. I picked up a framed photo of Kathy.

Her smile was as radiant as ever, her eyes filled with the same love and laughter that filled my dreams night after night since she left us.

I traced the outline of her face with my finger, my touch lingering on her lips. I could almost feel her warmth, her presence.

But she was gone.

Placing the framed photo back, I sank to my knees and closed my eyes. I prayed for strength. I prayed for guidance. I prayed for the courage to face each day without her.

Read more at https://karens-words.mailchimpsites.com.

Also by Karen Kazimer Shockley

Hearts United
Hearts United in Faith
Hearts United In Love
Hearts United in Love

Write. Publish. Thrive.
Secrets of Writing & Publishing

Watch for more at https://karens-words.mailchimpsites.com.

About the Author

Karen Kazimer Shockley was raised with an almost overwhelming amount of religious exposure. Karen began a journey to use this information to bring religion to a place where it was real in her life. This process reached critical mass when she met a wonderful man who embodied the true Christian life, without structured religion. Through his influence, she began to recognize spiritual presences in her own life. Her goal is to share these experiences with others so that they, too, can continue their journey to spiritual peace.

Read more at https://karens-words.mailchimpsites.com/.

www.ingramcontent.com/pod-product-compliance
Lightning Source LLC
Chambersburg PA
CBHW051131160726
47997CB00018B/1167